This book belongs to

....

Think Green!

by Jeanine Behr Getz

Illustrated by Jenny Nightingale

A portion of the proceeds from this book will be donated to eco-friendly causes
Published by Kids Think Big LLC
www.kidsthinkbig.com

Think Green!

Copyright © 2008 by Jeanine Behr Getz

Published in the United States of America by Kids Think Big LLC

Library of Congress Control Number: 2007906887

ISBN 978-0-9797362-0-9

Illustrated by Jenny Nightingale - www.jennynightingale.co.uk
Printed and bound in the United States of America

February 2008 First Edition

Kids Think Big LLC hopes to bring big ideas to children, via eco-friendly print
and electronic media, and empower them with knowledge at every age.
Never underestimate the power of children, their will to help,
their desire to learn or their need to understand.

Thank you to my husband Robert,
my daughter and parents
for always encouraging me,
and to my friends who inspired me,
especially John H. & Laura P.

My friends and I want to help keep the earth green and clean so we can all enjoy swimming in the ocean, watching animals in their natural habitats and breathing fresh air...

So we thought of green ways to help...

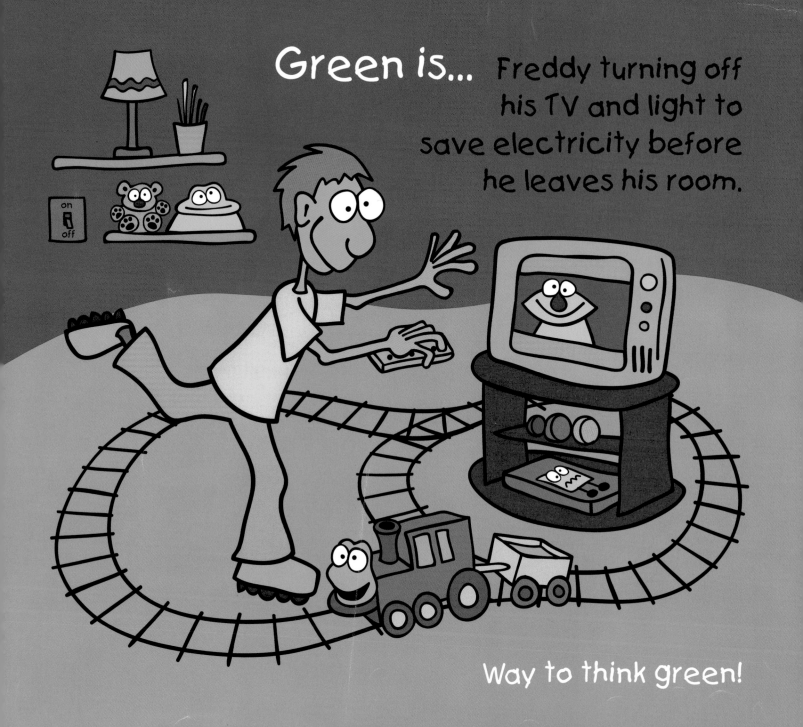

Green is... Freddy turning off his TV and light to save electricity before he leaves his room.

Way to think green!

cardboard & paper

metal

COMPOST
food &
garden
waste

Green is...
Caitlyn helping her family recycle.

glass

clothes

plastic

What a good green idea!

Green is...

Michael and his friends carpooling to school together, and Emily taking the school bus.

Great green teamwork!

Green is...
Kevin and Sarah picking up
litter when they see it and putting it
in the right place.

Litter thrown on the ground, in the water
or on the roads can hurt animals, fish and birds.

Great green teamwork!

Green is...
Andrew riding his bike
or walking to his friend's
house instead of
being driven in a car.

Now Andrew is
thinking green!

Green is...
Ryan using rechargeable batteries in his toys.
That's a great green idea!

Green is...

Georgia saving energy
by quickly closing the
refrigerator door after
she takes her apple.

Now Georgia is thinking green!

Green is...
James drinking water from a fountain rather than from plastic bottles.

Great green thinking!

Green is...
Nicole saving trees by giving
Ignacio a book and
birthday card made from
post consumer paper.

Way to think green!

Green is...

Jacob giving away the toys and clothes he no longer uses.

Good green idea!

Green is... Charlotte and Christian watching animals in their natural habitats...

...but not disturbing them.

How many ideas can you
and your friends
think of to
keep our world
green
and
clean?

Add them
to this book
on the
following
page.

Our green ideas...

Even a small group of thoughtful kids can think big and change the world!*

Keep thinking and acting GREEN!

*Millicent's adaptation of Maragret Mead